Also by Eve Ainsworth:

Because of You

Just Another Little Lie

KNOW my PLACE

Eve Ainsworth

Barrington Stoke

First published in 2021 in Great Britain by
Barrington Stoke Ltd
18 Walker Street, Edinburgh, EH3 7LP

www.barringtonstoke.co.uk

Text © 2021 Eve Ainsworth

A CIP catalogue record for this book is available
from the British Library upon request

ISBN: 978-1-78112-980-7

Printed by Hussar Books, Poland

To Kate
You are so special. Never forget it.
Thank you for being my life support.

ONE

BEFORE

I was ten years old when I met my last foster family, the Gibsons – Mary and her daughter, Stephanie.

I was scared and shy as I stood in Mary's living room. I had a sore, twisty stomach and a head full of worries. Mary took my small hand in hers and gripped it. She was tall, with bright red hair heaped on top of her head in a messy bun. Her eyes were sparkly, and her wide red lips seemed to stretch right across her face when she smiled.

"You're home now, Amy," Mary said. "We are going to look after you."

I looked around her large, cluttered living room. The shelves were packed with books and the cabinets stuffed full of interesting ornaments.

"I collect things," Mary explained. "Precious things, pretty things. And now I have another gem to add to my collection."

I didn't feel much like a gem as I stood there in my old jeans and jacket I'd outgrown. Mary didn't seem to notice that and took me on a tour of the house. She pointed out the old paintings hanging on the walls and apologised for the amount of "stuff" she had in each room.

"I've saved the best room until last," Mary said, pushing open the door.

I stood back, almost too afraid to step inside. The room was bigger than any bedroom I'd had before. The bed seemed lost inside it. I ran to the window. The view was stunning, overlooking the fields behind the house.

"Do you like your room?" Mary asked.

"It's perfect," I said.

Because it was.

Stephanie came home after school. She was just over a year older than me but at least 15 cm taller. Stephanie had the same colour hair as her mum, but it was styled neatly into a plait. She looked me up and down carefully and I saw her eyes were different to Mary's – cool and grey.

"We're going to be best friends," Stephanie said finally.

My first mistake was believing her.

NOW

There's a game I play in my head when things are difficult. It's pretty simple. There aren't many rules. No one knows I do it and I would hate for anyone to find out. They might laugh at me or see me for the silly idiot I really am. But the game helps me. I can believe that I'm someone else for a moment, that I'm normal. I pretend that everything is going to turn out fine.

I call the game "happy families", and I'm playing it right now in the car. I'm sitting in the back and if I slump a bit, I can just see the top of the driver's head. I can only make out a tuft of my new social worker's blonde hair and her black sparkly clip. It makes it easier to play the game. I close my eyes and let my imagination take over.

I can turn my life into someone else's.

I can make my life better.

You're my mum, I tell myself. *My real mum. You're driving me home. This clean, sweet-smelling car is all ours. At the weekend we will go food shopping. I will help you pick all our meals. We will giggle at some of the disgusting things in the supermarket – cabbage! Who even eats that?! We'll go clothes shopping despite me already having a wardrobe stuffed full of outfits. I have everything. Even a dad. He's—*

"Amy," says my social worker, Clare. "This is it. We're here."

I sit up. My eyes flutter open and the dream is broken. Reality is back, like a nasty twist in my stomach. I taste something bitter in my throat. I have to cough it away.

"Look! Look, Amy," Clare says. "This is your new home."

Clare's voice is sweet, upbeat. She presses her face into the space between the front seats to look at me. She is very pretty, like the china doll that used to live at the Gibsons', my last foster family. Clare's face is perfectly made up, with blusher highlighting her sharp cheekbones. Her blue eyes are large and clear under long eyelashes. She looks as fragile as the doll at the Gibsons', but is she really? Maybe Clare's tougher than that. Mary Gibson cried when I smashed that stupid china doll after I'd had another argument with Stephanie. Mary told me it was an expensive collectable. She was very upset with me for breaking it.

I don't know much about Clare except that I'm one of her "cases". I've had so many social workers before Clare, it's easy to lose count. They never really get to know me, apart from what they read in my file. I wonder what they think of me. A poor young girl abandoned by her mum and then shoved in the care system at the age of six after living with her poorly nan. My social workers must've been so pleased when they found the Gibsons. After all, that was meant to be my happy ending, my final page in the file.

I wonder if everyone blames me for it all going wrong. I bet they do. But they don't understand what it was like for me.

Clare has a posh voice and really smart high-heeled shoes. I can imagine her life is completely different from mine.

What's your family like, Clare? I want to ask but don't. *Do you have a nice mum? Not like me. But you know everything about me already, don't you? That's all I am, after all – a collection of recordings, a file of writing that is meant to tell the reader everything about me. But really it tells them nothing at all.*

The social worker I had before Clare was called Fiona. She was always snappy and in a hurry, seeing me as an irritation she could do without. Fiona never looked me in the eye and she always rushed our meetings. I didn't like her much at all.

I was never told what happened to Fiona. I assume she found a better job, perhaps with easier clients.

It wouldn't be the first time that's happened. I think I've had more than nine social workers and none have lasted over a year.

"Amy," Clare says again more firmly. She drums her fingers on the back of the seat. "Aren't you going to look at the house? It's very nice."

I shrug.

Clare sighs softly and moves to open her door. "I know you must be nervous, Amy," she says gently. But she knows nothing about it. Nothing at all. "It's never easy when a placement breaks down, but what happened at the Gibsons'—"

"Placement?" I repeat the word. It's such an odd, formal way to describe the place that had been my home for the past three years. But I guess that's all I am: something to be placed somewhere, like a piece of furniture. I'm unwanted and unloved, but I must be put somewhere so that I don't make any trouble. I wonder what will happen to me eventually. Where do the unwanted things go?

"'Placement' is just the term we use," Clare says, looking back at me. Her smile stretches across her face. It looks tiring. Her face muscles must hurt by the end of the day.

"We are hoping this will be a permanent home for you, Amy," Clare goes on. "The Dawsons really are a lovely family and they are so excited to have you. Kenny, their son, is only a year older than you and he's ever so nice."

I don't reply. I met my new foster parents, Gemma and Graham Dawson, briefly in the flurry of meetings to arrange this whole thing, but I haven't yet met Kenny. Everyone has told me how lovely and kind he is, but I'm not buying it. I was told the same things about Stephanie three years ago and look what happened there.

"Amy," Clare says. "Won't you just look? See for yourself. It's such a perfect house."

I sigh loudly, reach for the car door and open it. My body is stiff as I move out into the open. We are parked on a small drive. To the right is a shiny red BMW that looks freshly cleaned.

I look up. The house is detached and made of red brick with a large white garage attached. I glance at the plant pots dotted neatly under the front window, and at the gravel path winding towards a modern black front door with glass panels. Two small potted trees stand at each side of the door, twisted into shape like upright snakes.

"Nice," I mutter.

Posh, I think to myself.

"Isn't it?" Clare says. "I told you you'd like it."

"Yeah ..." I scuff at the ground. My trainers are old and shabby. They look out of place on this neat drive.

Clare moves behind me, to the car boot. She begins to search for my belongings. "We're a bit early," she says. "I didn't expect the journey to be so fast, but I'm sure it won't be a problem."

"I hope not," I reply. My gaze is fixed on the front door as I watch it open. A figure steps out into the sun, her hand held up in greeting.

Gemma Dawson.

My new mum.

I choke back a laugh.

Here we go again.

Another new home for Amy.

Inside, the house is white, clean and minimal. Gemma leads us into the living room first. The sofas are huge and covered in cushions that look expensive. I hang back by the door, studying the wooden statues and massive TV. A lot of stuff in here looks like it could break easily.

"We are so glad you're finally here," Gemma says softly.

I stare back at her. She is smaller than I remember, probably only a couple of centimetres taller than me. Her hair is dark, short and pushed away from her face. Her eyes are brown and remind me of conkers. She's staring at me so hard I feel like she can see right into me. My hands grip the bag I'm holding.

"Where's Graham?" Clare asks. "I'm guessing Kenny is still at school."

Gemma nods. "Kenny's at computer club until four thirty and Graham is planning to come home early from work." Gemma looks at me again. "You remember we told you that he's a teacher? He works at a private school across town. He's looking forward to seeing you again. We thought perhaps we could get a takeaway tonight?"

Clare almost squeals with excitement. "Oh, that sounds lovely, don't you think, Amy?"

I shrug. I guess so.

"I'm not that hungry," I say.

Gemma smiles. "It's OK," she says. "You don't have to eat much. Is there anything you fancy? Kenny loves pizza."

"I don't mind," I say, and hold her gaze. I want Gemma to see that I'm not some six year old that can be won over with treats. I know how it all works. I'm tired of playing games. "I'll eat whatever really."

"Good." Gemma's voice is still bright. Her eyes break away from me and sweep over my bags. I can almost hear what she's thinking – *not much stuff.* I suppose I don't have much. Some clothes. A few books that I've kept over the years. I didn't really get many new things when I lived with the Gibsons, especially near the end. There wasn't much point when I hardly left my room.

"Perhaps I should show you around," Gemma says. "We really want you to feel at home here, Amy."

Clare nudges me and says, "That sounds like a great idea. Go on, Amy, have a good look about. Get familiar with the place." She pauses, then adds, "I'm going to go now, Amy. But I'll be back soon. To check everything is OK. And you have my number. You can call me if you need to."

Clare stares at me for a moment or two and then a soft smile flutters across her face.

"Go on, Amy. It'll be all right," Clare says. "You'll get settled in no time. You'll see."

Settled? I glare back at Clare. Is she being serious?

Clare doesn't notice my mood, or if she does, she chooses to ignore it. She just nods gently.

Gemma goes to show Clare back out. I have no option but to stay where I am for the moment. My arms are stiff at my sides and my stomach is twisted, dreading what's to come.

Clare turns back to me briefly. "It'll be OK," she says again. Her smile is gone. She is serious. "Trust me."

I almost laugh.

I was right about Clare. She's just like the other social workers. She really doesn't understand.

TWO

BEFORE

Stephanie was my new sister. At first everything was fine. We watched TV together and she sometimes let me read her books. Stephanie even showed me how her cat, Molly, liked to be stroked. But at the same time she warned me that Molly was *her* cat and shouldn't be stroked without permission.

I didn't mind that. For a while I let myself believe that things were going to be OK.

But as time went by there were little things that made me think Stephanie might not really want to be my friend. Soon she seemed to become bored of me. I was no longer a new, interesting thing. Instead, I was a pain. Someone who was simply in the way. Stephanie started to make comments when Mary wasn't listening.

"I don't like your clothes much," she said once, looking me up and down. "And you're so skinny. All bony. It's a bit weird."

So I wore my baggiest clothes and tried to hide my small, thin body from her hard gaze.

"You dress all old-fashioned," Stephanie said one time. She laughed and pulled at my clothes.

I blushed. I felt like no matter what I did, I wasn't good enough in Stephanie's opinion.

"It's not your fault," she said. "You're just very different from me."

And I suppose that summed it up.

I was like a jigsaw piece in the wrong place. I wouldn't fit, no matter how much you tried to ram me into the space.

NOW

I follow Gemma as she shows me around the house.

"This is the kitchen, of course," Gemma says, and spreads out her arms. "You can help yourself to whatever you want. There's ice in the fridge and plenty of juice and milk. I keep chocolate and biscuits in the cupboard here." She taps a shiny white door. "I'm guessing I can trust you not to go mad."

"I won't," I say. "It's a really nice house."

Gemma smiles. "Thank you. We had an extension built last year." She walks over to the island in the centre of the kitchen. It has high white stools around it. "I like cooking – baking especially. Do you?"

My mind flutters briefly. I think of a smaller kitchen long ago, of making pastry on a tiny chipped wooden table with Nan. My fingers were caked in gooey mess and there was flour on my clothes and face. Nan kept laughing as I moved the dough around, stretching it out like it was play dough.

"Watch it, love," Nan said. "You'll get it everywhere. Silly thing ..."

I think of later times, in the Gibsons' cluttered kitchen. Mary was watching as I mixed up the cake batter, her face bright with happiness.

"You're really good at this, Amy," Mary said. "I'm impressed ..."

"No," I say finally to Gemma, my voice sharp. "I don't like baking. Not now anyway."

I walk across the clean slate tiles towards the wide glass doors that lead out to the garden. I press my face up to the glass.

"Wow. It's huge," I say.

I think it's the biggest garden I've ever seen. The grass seems to go on for ever and large trees line the bottom. There is a swing seat to the side of the grass and smart patio furniture set out just in front of me.

"We like to eat out there when the weather is warmer," Gemma says, coming up behind me. "Graham does an amazing barbeque."

"I've never had a barbeque before," I say. I think of the Gibsons' tiny garden, messy and full of flower tubs and garden ornaments. Mary liked to sit outside with a cup of tea and watch the birds eat stale bread from her overgrown grass. Mary used to joke that barbeques were for "posh people" and that she didn't have time for things like that.

Gemma pauses before saying, "Well, that's something we can change."

We stand for a moment longer, just looking out. It's so clean and tidy out there, completely different to what I'm used to. There's so much space.

"Amy?" Gemma says. "Perhaps you'd like to see your room now?"

I nod. I would.

Suddenly I feel very tired.

Gemma leads me into the tidy hallway. I notice shoes lined up on a small wooden stand. White trainers, black ankle boots, a neat pair of Nike high tops.

"It's very tidy," I say.

"It's not always like this," Gemma laughs. "I had a big clean-up before you came. I wanted to impress you."

"Really?" I say. I'm not sure I believe her. "It's a bit different from my last home."

Gemma gestures towards the stairs, meaning that I should go first. "Is it? How?" Gemma asks.

"Well, I guess it was smaller there ..." I start. She nods, signalling I should continue as we head up the stairs. "It was OK. Cosy. But the house was packed full of stuff. Mary used to say that she didn't have the patience to be cleaning all the time. It was just Mary and her daughter, Stephanie."

I freeze at the thought of Stephanie's last cold, unblinking stare. I remember her harsh words as I left the Gibsons' home for the last time: *"Don't hurry back ..."*

Stephanie really had been awful. I wasn't upset to leave her, that's for sure. But I think of Mary's sad face and her tearful eyes as she said goodbye and I feel a tug of regret. I wish, more than anything else, that I hadn't hurt Mary.

"I'm sorry it didn't work out, Amy," Gemma says.

I shrug. "It doesn't matter."

"I heard that Mary got ill ..."

I stare at Gemma, feeling heat rise inside my body. "If it's OK, I'd rather not talk about it," I say.

Gemma nods. "Of course," she says gently.

There's no way I want to tell her about it all. Not yet anyway. Mary Gibson said I couldn't stay because she was too tired and ill. She said she couldn't cope with fostering any more but that it wasn't my fault.

But I know different. I know if I had been a nicer, easier girl, Mary would have kept me. If I hadn't argued with Stephanie all the time, it would've been OK. I'm sure the illness was just Mary's excuse to get rid of me.

I pause on the stairs. Photos line the wall beside me. There's a shot of Gemma and Graham on their wedding day. He's tall and strong looking, standing proudly, with dark blond hair that seems too spiky to touch. He has a broad smile. Gemma is dressed in a long, fitted white dress. Her hair is longer – dark curls bouncing around her neck.

"I was a lot younger there," Gemma says. She seems shy, a smile twitching at her lips. "It was a very special day."

My gaze drifts to the next photo. A boy is with them in this one. Small with a tuft of messy, mousey hair. He squints at the camera as if looking directly at the sun.

"That's Kenny, before he got his glasses," Gemma explains. "Look, here's a more recent one." Gemma reaches across and touches a large framed picture. It's a school photo. Kenny sits facing the camera, his hair soft and brushed away from his face. His smile is shy and awkward. Dark glasses frame his light blue eyes.

"You'll like Kenny once you get to know him," Gemma says. "Everyone does."

I nod. I don't really know what else to say. The wall is covered with faces – more people that I do not know. They are all smiling at me with bright eyes. It's pretty overwhelming.

"Maybe soon I can put your picture up there," Gemma says.

I flinch. I don't mean to, but her words are like a whip that hits old wounds.

Mary hung my picture up in her house. She placed it proudly beside Stephanie's. Two girls in their school uniforms smiling brightly. Two girls who looked so happy.

"There – how perfect is that?" Mary said, stroking the frame. "My two daughters."

I expect my photo has been taken down now. I wonder if it's left a faded mark on the wall. Or maybe another picture of Stephanie has been hung in its place, removing me for ever.

"It's OK," Gemma says, her hand pressing on the bannister. "No rush, eh? There's no need to rush anything. Let me show you your room now. The most important part."

We carry on walking, reaching the landing in silence. Gemma directs me gently to the first room on the right. The door is already open.

"I hope you like it," she says. "I hope we got it right."

I hold back a choke in my throat.

It's beautiful.

She couldn't have got it more wrong.

It's too perfect. All of it.

The carpet is soft and grey and sinks around my tatty trainers as I step inside. The bed is huge. I think it might be a double. It is covered in clean white bedding and bright cushions. The walls are plain white but decorated with large bright prints – two are colourful abstract art and one is of a wolf cub.

"We knew you liked art. And wolves," Gemma says softly. "But you can change anything you like. This was just to start it off."

There is a large white dressing table in the corner, a wardrobe, a table with a TV and a huge bookcase stuffed full of books.

"They're mainly Kenny's books," Gemma says. "I'm sorry it's mostly sci-fi and horror, but we can stock up on others. I know you like to read."

"To escape …" I mutter.

Gemma doesn't seem to hear me. "We can go shopping any time. Get you some new things. I thought that might be nice." She opens the wardrobe. I see there is stuff already hanging there. "I ordered some basic things in your size. Jeans and T-shirts. Nothing much."

"I have all I need already," I tell her.

Gemma nods. "OK, that's fine, but they're there if you change your mind."

My hands are clenched in tight balls. I try to let go. I try to relax as Gemma continues to talk. She points out the bathroom, tells me I can shower or bathe whenever I want. She shows me where my personal towels are, fluffy and white and new.

"Shall I leave you to settle in?" Gemma asks. "Graham will be home soon. We can catch up again then."

That word again – settle. God, how I hate it. I nod, feeling numb. I watch how Gemma backs out of the room, her smile nervous and unsure. She wants me to be happy. She wants me to like it here.

I'm not sure that can ever be possible.

THREE

BEFORE

Mary Gibson was lovely. She was loud and topsy-turvy. She sang as she baked in the kitchen. I would sit and watch her at the kitchen table, staring at her busy hands as she rolled out the dough. She reminded me so much of someone else.

"What are you thinking about, love?" Mary asked me. "You seem lost in thought."

"My nan used to bake too," I said. "Sometimes I'd help her."

"Ah." Mary didn't say anything more, but she studied me with wide, kind eyes. She knew what had happened of course – with my nan and why I had ended up in foster care.

"You can help me if you like?" Mary offered, holding out the rolling pin. "Get this pastry nice and smooth for me. If I'm honest, I've never been much good at it."

I took the rolling pin keenly and began to press out the dough. The fresh scent of flour dusted my nose. I pictured Nan next to me, telling me to "iron out all the bumps". I could smell Nan's fresh lavender scent and hear her soft throaty chuckle.

Nan was the only person who had ever loved me.

But now she was gone.

Mary touched my hand gently. "That's perfect," she said. "I can see you have a knack for this. You and I are going to have to do more baking together. Stephanie can never be bothered. It'll be nice to have someone to do it with."

"I'd love that," I replied.

But as I looked up I saw Stephanie standing silently behind Mary in the doorway. She was staring right at me.

And she looked like she hated me.

NOW

I sit on the bed and look around me. This is meant to be my room, but I'm not sure it will be for long. It's just another passing place. Somewhere for me to rest my head until it all goes wrong. I'll soon be moved away from here. I'm moved away from everywhere in the end.

When I was young, I lived with my nan – but she died when I was six. Since then, I've had five different bedrooms in five different homes. The first two were temporary – places for me to stay while social services worked out what to do with me. Then I was moved to a family called the Foxes. I was eight, and already tired of moving homes. I wanted my nan back. No one else. Everything felt so wrong. I lasted just over a year with the Foxes before the social worker said that the placement wasn't right for me.

So then I had another temporary home, and after a few months I was moved to the Gibsons'. Everyone was excited about that placement. My social worker back then told me she had a good feeling about it.

My room at the Gibsons' was cosy and bright. Like Gemma Dawson, Mary had got books and clothes for me. She gave me a phone. She made an effort.

I started to hope things would be OK.

But it only lasted three years. So here I am in a new room – my sixth.

Aged thirteen. Waiting for it all to go wrong again.

I shove my bags into the bottom of the wardrobe. I don't see any point in unpacking them. But I do pull out my favourite book and my writing journal. I take them both to my bedside table and place them there. The book was my nan's – she gave it to me when I was living with her. It's *The Lion, the Witch and the Wardrobe*. I don't read this type of book normally, but there is something about this one that is special. I have read it so many times that the pages are worn and creased, and the cover is becoming tatty. But I don't care. I will keep it for ever. I wish I could escape to Narnia, to another world where animals love and care for you and where brave creatures can be brought back to life.

I stroke the book's cover and blink back the tears that are fighting to get out. I will not cry. I cannot.

If I start crying now, I might never stop.

I hear the front door open and close and then there are loud voices. I think it's Graham arriving home. I get up off the bed and walk to the door. Gently, I ease it open. I can hear Graham and Gemma talking, but I can't hear their exact words. My mind whirs as I wonder what they are saying.

Mary and Stephanie used to talk about me, at the end of my time there.

They probably thought I couldn't hear them, but I could. I would press my ear up to the wall in my room and hear them muttering next door in Stephanie's room.

Stephanie would complain about me and Mary would try to soothe her. I knew that, despite her kindness, Mary always tended to believe Stephanie.

After all, Stephanie was her daughter.

I was the outsider.

I hear footsteps on the stairs and dash back to my bed. There is a gentle knock on my door.

"Come in," I call quietly.

Graham eases open the door but stays on the threshold. He smiles at me. "Hey, Amy. It's good to see you again."

Graham looks like I remember from when we briefly met before – very tall, with a face that almost seems elastic. His smile forms easily, and his eyes are bright and friendly.

I smile back shyly, feeling so awkward. Even sitting here on the bed feels wrong. I am so out of place.

"We were hoping that you might want to come downstairs," Graham says. "Kenny will be home soon. I know he's been looking forward to meeting you."

"OK." I nod.

I follow Graham out of the room, carefully shutting the door behind me.

I'm a bit nervous about meeting Kenny. I'm not sure we will have that much in common. Apparently, he's into computers and chess. He sounds like a bit of a geek if I'm honest. Not that that matters.

I probably won't know him for long.

FOUR

BEFORE

"She'll never be your mum, you know," Stephanie said.

I'd been living at the Gibsons' for a year now and Stephanie and I were walking to school together for the first time. I was moving up to her secondary school and I was feeling a bit nervous.

I'd liked my primary school. Yes, I was shy and hadn't made many friends, but it had been somewhere to escape from Stephanie for a bit. She pretended that everything was fine when Mary was around – it was only when we were on our own that she treated me like I was an annoying pest.

And now Stephanie and I would be in the same school together. I wasn't sure how I felt about that.

Mary had said goodbye to us both with a light kiss on the cheek. She had ruffled my hair gently and told me to "have a good day". Mary said I wasn't to worry because Stephanie would be there to make sure I was all right. Stephanie was already settled in Year Eight, so she could look after me.

But Stephanie didn't seem very happy about this. "You mustn't show me up in school," she said now, her eyes scanning me up and down. "Are you even going to get a haircut any time soon?"

My hand fluttered to my head, touching the long strands that fell down my back. Nan had always said my hair was my best feature. She said I should never cut it and that I should keep growing it like Rapunzel.

And then Stephanie said those awful words: "She'll never be your mum." The words fell from her lips so casually. Her eyes scanned mine like she was waiting for a reaction. "My mum just feels sorry for you, that's all. She thinks she's doing something nice, but I can tell she's already getting tired of you."

"Tired of me?" I said, my eyes widening. "Is she?"

"Of course." Stephanie giggled. "A dull little thing like you. Why wouldn't she? You're not what we hoped you would be."

What could I even say to that? My gaze dropped back down to the pavement and my throat began to tighten.

That was the first time I realised that my "forever home" was at risk.

NOW

Kenny comes home at five o'clock. He crashes into the house and rushes to the living room, where I'm already sitting. Then he stands in the doorway, looking awkwardly at me, as if he's not exactly sure what to say.

"Hi," I say.

"Hi," Kenny replies, and holds out his hand in a half wave. "You're here then?" He smiles.

"Yeah. I'm here."

"Where are my parents?" Kenny asks.

"I think your dad is ordering food and your mum is making some tea."

"Tea?" Kenny says, wrinkling his nose. "Do you really like that stuff?"

I shrug. "It's OK, I guess."

I take the chance to stare a bit at Kenny. He looks a lot like his photo. His hair is very soft and mousey and brushed away from his face. His glasses are large with dark frames. His mouth is small and his smile seems unsure, as if he's trying to work me out.

"So – how do you like it here?" Kenny asks.

"I've only just arrived," I reply. "It seems OK."

"Mum and Dad aren't so bad," Kenny says, and pushes his glasses up. "I mean – they can be a bit annoying at times, but on the whole they are pretty chilled out about most stuff."

"Oh," I say. "That's cool." I glance down at my lap and brush off an invisible crumb. "I was told that you like computers."

"Yeah?" Kenny seems to brighten. "Do you? I like gaming and coding mostly."

I shake my head. "Nah. It's not really my thing. Sorry."

He shifts on the spot, clearly feeling a bit more uncomfortable. "Oh, well, that's fine ..." Kenny says. "But if you ever wanted to—"

"I won't," I interrupt. "But thanks."

I can't pretend that I'm into the same things as him, and I'm not even sure there is much point in trying. After all, look what happened when I started to think that Stephanie might be OK.

I sigh loudly. "Was there anyone else before me then?"

Kenny frowns a bit. "What do you mean? A foster kid?"

"Yeah," I say.

"No. You're the first."

"Oh."

I'm not sure what to think of this. Do Graham and Gemma understand what this all involves? Are they looking for a perfect daughter to fill a gap in their lives? Because if that's the case, I'm not sure I can be that person.

As if on cue, Gemma and Graham both breeze into the room.

"Oh, lovely!" Gemma says. Her hands are clutching an old-fashioned tea tray. "I didn't realise you were home, Kenny."

Graham walks over to him, claps his arm. "You OK, mate? I see you've met Amy."

"Yes. Yes, I have," Kenny replies in a low voice. "It's nice to finally have her here." He flashes me a nervous smile, then quietly leaves the room.

Graham has ordered pizza. He tells me not to worry about Kenny. He says that Kenny is just nervous and wants to make the right impression.

I shrug. I've heard this all before.

"Kenny's used to being on his own," Gemma explains. "But he's lovely – really friendly. You have nothing to worry about."

"Was Kenny OK about all of this?" I ask carefully. My thoughts flick back to Stephanie. "I mean, I don't even know why you guys decided to foster."

Gemma nods. "Oh yes, Kenny was consulted all the way, don't you worry. He is as keen as us for this to work." She pauses and looks briefly at Graham. "We always wanted a bigger family – and when it was clear that couldn't happen because of medical reasons, we decided we wanted to expand our family in other ways. As you know, Graham is a teacher, and I work in a nursery. We like being around children. We want to open our home to someone new – to you."

"Kenny has always said it's a good thing to do," Graham adds gently. "We wouldn't have done this if he didn't want to."

I think of Stephanie. I wonder how much Mary had spoken to her about fostering me. Maybe she hadn't – and maybe that was why it had gone wrong.

"But why me? Why a teenager?" I ask.

"Why not?" Graham smiles. "I work with teenagers and we wanted someone close to Kenny in age. It seemed like a good fit for us."

A good fit? Is that what I am? Like a pair of shoes? I look at both Graham and Gemma and see how they are gazing at me, waiting for a reaction. I swallow dry air and force myself to smile.

"I hope I am," I say.

But doubts are flooding through me like a river.

By the time the pizza arrives, Kenny has come back downstairs. To be fair, he seems pretty friendly, but I can't help worrying that he's pretending. It all seems so easy for him – how he chats to his parents, how he moves around the kitchen to get a drink. I bet he's never felt out of place or unwelcome in his life.

Everyone makes a big fuss about the pizza, saying how it's from the best place in town. Gemma hands me a box and I open it to find the biggest pizza I have ever seen. I swear my stomach shrinks at the sight of it. I think the nerves and stress of everything have stolen my appetite. I nibble the edges of my pizza and watch while the family talk, trying to figure them all out.

It's pretty clear that Gemma is in charge of things here. She leads the conversation. Graham is more of an observer, sitting back and letting everyone else get on with it. But every so often he'll make a witty comment or slip in a joke.

And then there's Kenny. I still can't work him out. I thought he was awkward and shy at first, but now he seems at ease, telling his mum about his school day, joking with his dad about the "annoying popular kids" and eating his pizza fast, as if he's starving.

"Amy," Gemma says, interrupting my thoughts. "Are you OK? You seem very quiet. Is this a bit much for you?"

I shake my head. "I'm fine," I reply.

"But you've hardly eaten." Gemma points at my pizza box. "Don't you like it?"

"I love it," I say. Because I do. But I can't tell her about the heaviness in my stomach. How it makes my appetite so small. She'll never get it.

"You should try and eat a bit more," Gemma says softly. "It might make you feel better."

"I feel fine."

"Leave Amy be, Gemma," Graham says, half laughing. "Honestly, don't make a fuss."

"She just looks a bit pale," Gemma replies. "I'm sorry, Amy. Am I being a bit full-on? I have this tendency to want to feed people up." She giggles nervously.

I do not giggle back.

I've always been thin. Everyone that's looked after me has tried to fill me up like I'm some kind of stuffed toy. Even Nan tried with her cakes and homemade biscuits. Nobody understands that you can't fill up someone who's already full. My body isn't full of food but stuffed up with worry and fear.

"It might take a while, Amy, but I want you to feel relaxed around us," Gemma says. "We're here for the long run. We want to help you."

My body stiffens. I push away the pizza box. "You can't say that," I tell her.

Gemma nods. Her smile is like a painted mask. "Yes. Yes, I can."

"No," I say, and stand up, knocking the kitchen stool sideways. "You can't say that. Everyone has said it to me. Everyone before. They all want to help. They all want to be there for me, and they never are."

Graham leans towards me. "What do you want right now, Amy?" he asks.

"I just want to be left alone."

"OK, that's fine," Graham replies. "We understand. We really do."

I'm back in the bedroom, the room that is meant to be mine. I lie down on my bed and try not to cry. I will not weaken. Not here. Not again.

The room seems smaller now and I'm struggling to breathe. I have to close my eyes and focus. I do what I always do when I feel like this. I play my pretend game again.

Except this time, I'm back in the best place of all.

I'm back with my nan.

I pretend she's downstairs baking. If I focus hard enough, I can smell fresh bread. I can hear Nan singing. It's an old song, something that was number one a hundred years ago, and Nan's voice is loud and out of tune, but I don't care. To me it sounds wonderful.

I pretend I'm back with my nan and everything is OK again.

I pretend I'm safe.

I pick up my journal and write. I try to write in it as often as I can. It's my release. When I write in it, I imagine I'm writing to Nan and I tell her about the things I'm finding hard. It makes me feel connected to her. I can almost imagine Nan sitting next to me.

It's a nice house, Nan. But it's not like ours. It's so new and modern, and I'm scared that if I touch something, I might break it. What would they think then, eh? They would be bound to get cross with me.

I don't belong here with my old clothes and my hair that needs cutting. I must look such a mess to them. I'm trying to be polite, because I know that's what you would want me to do – but I'm scared to relax. If I start to do that, it could go all wrong.

It's best I don't expect too much. At least that way no one will be disappointed.

All I want is to find a home where I belong again. Like I did with you.

FIVE

BEFORE

Grange Secondary School was so much bigger than my old primary school. My class was busy and loud. I sat next to a girl called Rebecca. She had long blonde hair and a pretty face. Rebecca was nice to me, but she already had three friends here from her old school. She didn't understand why I was so shy and didn't feel like talking much. There were girls from my primary school here, but I wasn't very friendly with them. They were much more confident than me and fitted in easily. As usual, I found it easier to just blend into the background.

During my first breaktime at the school I searched for Stephanie, thinking it might help.

I was hoping she might be nice to me like Mary had promised. Stephanie was sitting on the benches by the lunch hall. As soon as she saw me, her face hardened.

"You shouldn't be here," Stephanie said as her friends giggled behind her. "You're in Year Seven. You should be with your lot."

"But Mary said you would look out for me," I said.

Stephanie flapped a hand at me. "My mum didn't mean that. She says things she doesn't mean all the time." Her eyes glinted. "I told you I didn't want you showing me up."

I felt my insides opening up, like there was a huge hole inside me letting all the icy air in.

"I don't want you around me all the time, do you get it?" Stephanie hissed. "I've been pretending before. I just did it to please my mum, but now I'm sick of you. You're always in the way, trying to suck up to my mum, just because you haven't got one. And now you're here, at my school, getting under my feet."

"I ..." I started to say, but I didn't have the words. Stephanie laughed instead.

"You have no one, Amy," she said. "No one wants you."

That was the day when everything changed.

NOW

My first week at the Dawsons' passes by. It's not so bad, but it's also not great. I manage to get into a kind of routine. Eating breakfast, going back to my room. Coming out for lunch and dinner, and sometimes sitting in the garden if I can face it.

Gemma and Graham don't push me. They tell me they are here for me if I need them. They ask me if there is anywhere I want to go, but I tell them there isn't.

I don't see much of Kenny, as he's at school. When he is home, he mostly goes to his room too. Sometimes I hear him talking loudly on his computer microphone, probably to some other poor geek somewhere.

Gemma agrees that I don't have to start school until Monday, which I'm relieved about.

One of the things that stressed me out about moving here was the idea of beginning a new school. I don't think people realise how hard it is to start over. When you're eight or nine, being the new kid is cute and even pretty fun – everyone wants to be your friend. I know it won't be that way at secondary school. The other kids will be nosy. They will wonder what is wrong with me and why I had to change schools so late.

I'm not sure I'm ready to do all this.

On Friday, Gemma comes into my room and walks straight over to my bed. I'm lying on it trying to read *The Lion, the Witch and the Wardrobe* for the millionth time. But none of the words are sticking, and I'm reading the same line over and over again.

"Is that book good?" Gemma asks brightly. "I read it years ago but can hardly remember it now. I can just picture the lion – Aslan, isn't it?"

"Yeah. It's all right." I put the book down carefully beside me.

"It looks old," Gemma says. "Have you had it a long time?"

"Yeah ..."

She smiles. Her teeth are so perfectly straight and white.

"We have to go out today, Amy," Gemma says carefully, her eyes studying my face. "We need to pick up your school uniform from the shop in town. I want to make sure it all fits."

My stomach feels hollow. I shift on the bed. "Do we have to go today?" I ask.

"Well, yes. It's already a bit later than I'd planned. You start on Monday. I just hope everything is there ..."

"If not, maybe we can delay the start?" I say.

Gemma's eyes meet mine. She frowns slightly. "Well, maybe. We'd need to discuss that with the school." She pauses. "So, are you OK coming with me now?"

I consider it. I am bored, sitting here. The room is hot today and I can't focus on the book. I'd like to get out and see the town. Also, I want to see my uniform. What if some of it is missing? Or it doesn't fit? I would have the perfect excuse not to start the new school and none of it would be my fault.

"OK," I say.

*

Gemma drives us into town. The BMW is brand
new and smells of leather and polish. She puts on
the air conditioning as we pull away and cool air
blasts me from all directions. Even so, my legs
still feel sticky against the seat.

I stare out of the window as we drive, passing
along the wide, tidy streets into the main town.
This is a nice area. All the houses are large and
detached with sweeping drives and big, pretty
front gardens. I think of Nan's house, where
I lived when I was little – it was a tiny end of
terrace in the middle of a busy estate. I wonder
what it's like now. If there are other people living
there. Or if it's empty.

I hate to think of Nan's house like that.
Unloved and alone.

But I can totally relate.

The uniform shop is very small. The place
is packed with bright uniforms of all colours
hanging from racks.

The man behind the counter greets us. He is pretty old with a kind face. Gemma gives him my name and he goes out the back to collect her order. I stand behind Gemma, crossing my fingers, hoping that something will be wrong.

Sadly, nothing is.

The uniform is all there. Black skirt, white shirt and red and black tie. Gemma asks me to try it all on in the changing room, which I do in silence. I still hope that the clothes won't fit me, but as I stare back in the mirror it is clear that they do. I look like a stranger. A stranger in someone else's uniform. Someone who doesn't belong.

Gemma sweeps back the curtain.

"Oh, you look amazing," she says. "You'll fit right in."

It is all I can do not to cry.

Gemma takes me to a cafe afterwards. It's in another small shop in the same lane, just opposite the uniform shop. I sit and wait at the table while she orders drinks and cake for both of us. I told

Gemma I'm not really hungry, but I'm not sure she believes me. The bag full of uniform is resting between my legs. It feels heavy and awkward.

All I want to do is put my head on the table and close my eyes, but I know that will make me look even weirder. So I stare out of the window instead, watching as people walk past. It's getting busier now it's nearer lunchtime. I see people who look like they might be on their break from work, dressed in suits and walking in a rush. I see a group of older teenagers walking in a huddle and laughing loudly. Then I see an older lady clutching a young girl's hand. My mouth goes dry. I look away again.

"I ordered some of the homemade cake. It looks delicious," Gemma says, sitting down opposite me. "I got you a milkshake. I thought you deserved it. The lady will bring it over in a second."

"Thank you," I reply, and lick my lips.

Gemma leans towards me. "You're ever so quiet today, Amy. Is everything OK?"

I nod. "Of course."

She purses her lips a little. "Well, we've noticed you've been very quiet since you arrived." Gemma leans in closer and lowers her voice. "I know it must be so hard, Amy. This is new for us too. I guess we're all just finding our way, aren't we?" She pauses and spreads her hands out on the table. "I guess what I'm trying to say is, I understand that you might be feeling out of sorts, but I'm here if you ever want to talk."

Out of sorts? That's a new expression. I wonder when I was last "in sorts". I smile back at her anyway. "Thank you."

The waitress brings over a tray and I see the huge chocolate milkshake placed on top. I know that my social care notes say that I like chocolate milkshakes the best. I remember sitting with a social worker when I was about eight years old and listing my favourite things. Luckily this one hasn't changed.

The waitress places the milkshake in front of me with a bright smile. I take a long sip. It is ice cold and just the right level of chocolatey.

I look over at Gemma. "This is amazing," I say.

She laughs. "You have a chocolate moustache now."

I swipe at my face. But I don't care. This is the best thing I've tasted for months.

The waitress has returned, holding out another tray with two plates on top.

"What's that?" I ask.

The waitress smiles again and carefully places both plates in front of us. "Carrot cake. It's our most popular choice."

Gemma giggles and says, "I know it's naughty, but I couldn't resist."

I shake my head. "No. I can't eat that."

Gemma's eyes widen. "You don't like it? Amy, I'm sorry, I should've checked first. Is there anything else you want instead?"

I push the plate away. Sickness is swelling inside me. "You don't understand," I say. "I can't eat it. I don't want to see it. Please take it away."

It's impossible to stop the tears this time.

Gemma waits. The cake has been removed and she sits opposite me sipping her tea. Her face is concerned, but she doesn't speak. I like that. I don't want to be pushed into talking yet.

I wipe my eyes. I feel silly and embarrassed. I don't want the other customers to keep looking at me. I feel bad that I made such a fuss. They probably think that I'm a bad kid acting up, and my cheeks go hot at the thought.

"It's just the cake ..." I say finally. "Carrot cake. It makes me remember ..."

"It's OK, Amy," Gemma says. "You don't have to tell me unless you want to."

The memory is from years ago at my nan's, but I can still taste the carrot cake on my lips now. It's sweet with a hint of spice. So moist and fresh. I was chewing on the cake, enjoying every bite until I heard the crash in the kitchen. The crumbs were in my throat, trapped inside like dry dust when I found Nan on the floor. The cake was choking me.

"My nan," I say finally, my words sounding heavy. "She made carrot cake all the time. When I lived with her ..."

The last words hang between us. Gemma nods slowly.

"You must miss her very much," she says.

"I do."

"You were very young when she died, weren't you?"

"I was six," I say.

Gemma lowers her eyes. "I can't even begin to imagine ..." Her fingers touch the table in between us, but don't reach me. "Amy, if you ever want to talk about it, I'm here for you, OK?" Gemma pauses. "But I understand that might not be right now. I understand that it could be too hard. I'm here when you're ready."

I nod. "Thank you."

I can't tell her that it hurts so much and that just thinking of what happened to Nan makes me ache from the inside out. But I like the way Gemma isn't pushing me to talk or expecting too much of me. It makes me relax a bit.

"I promise I won't buy carrot cake again," she says. "Unless you want it, of course."

"Thank you," I say again. I manage a small smile.

The plates have gone now, and my milkshake sits unfinished. I should feel better. I sit back and take a small breath, trying to clear my thoughts.

In front of me there is a tiny crumb of cake on the table. I flick it off onto the floor.

I know I need to get better at dealing with this stuff.

I look back up at Gemma, at her warm, kind face. Could she be the one to help me do it?

SIX

BEFORE

I was sitting in front of the TV with Stephanie's cat, Molly, curled up on my lap. Outside it was raining, so it felt snug and warm inside the cosy living room. The programme was an American drama. I wasn't interested in it, but it was taking my mind off the thoughts inside my head.

Stephanie walked in and picked up the remote control. Without saying a word, she flicked the channel over.

"I was watching that," I said.

Stephanie said nothing – she simply sat on the chair opposite and stared at the screen.

I reached for the remote control, my insides churning, but Stephanie snatched it away from me.

"It's my TV, not yours," she said coldly. "I want to watch it now."

"Why are you being like this?" I asked.

"Like what?" Stephanie said, her gaze darting across to me. "This is my house. I can do what I want."

I wanted to say that it was my house too, but I looked at Stephanie's hard expression and felt the familiar tug of loneliness. There was no point.

Mary walked into the room clutching a cup of tea. She rubbed at her face. Her eyes were lined with dark shadows.

"Are you OK?" Mary asked. "Still getting along?"

"Oh, yes. We're getting on fine," Stephanie said sweetly. "Just watching our favourite programme together, aren't we, Amy?"

I didn't say a word.

NOW

When Gemma and I get back from the cafe, I sit in the living room watching some quiz show on TV with Graham. He seems to like it and gets really excited when he answers the question correctly. I can't help smiling when Graham punches the arm of the chair each time.

"Sorry," he says when he sees me watching. "I've not had such a winning streak on here for ages. I'm beginning to feel clever."

The thing is, Graham is clever. Really clever. It fascinates me to see how much he knows about so many subjects. I'm guessing he must be a really good teacher. And a good dad.

I never knew my dad, so I have no idea whether he is clever or not. He could be the prime minister for all I know. Mum ran off when I was a baby, and Nan was never able to find her. I think she got mixed up in a bad gang. Nan always said Mum "went off the rails" and I know Nan always worried about her. But no one knew about my dad – who he was, or even what he was like. He'll always be a mystery to me.

My thoughts are interrupted by Gemma bursting into the room.

"Hey, Amy," she says. "Come upstairs. We have a surprise for you."

I look back at her, confused, but Graham leans over and nudges me. "Go on, quick," he says. "I think you might like this."

I follow Gemma upstairs, feeling a bit tense. I'm not sure I like surprises much. Most of the surprises I've had have not been good ones.

Gemma leads me into my room and throws up her arms.

"Ta da!" she says.

In front of me, Kenny is kneeling by a new white desk, and on top of it is a laptop.

I blink at it, not able to believe it.

"Is that for me?" I ask.

"Of course it is," Kenny says, standing up. "I've set it up for you and sorted the Wi-Fi and everything."

I walk over to the laptop and gently run my fingers over the keys. They feel so soft. I had a computer at the Gibsons', but I shared it with Stephanie and she hardly let me on it. This is the first time I've ever had anything like this of my own.

"We thought you might want to do some writing on it," Gemma says gently. "Homework. Connect with friends?"

I shake my head. I don't have friends, not really. But it doesn't matter. It is still perfect.

"Thank you," I say, and I really mean it.

Kenny stays in my room to help me set up my email account.

"I'm guessing you have people you'll want to contact?"

I shrug and say, "Not really. I stopped going to my old school towards the end of the year, so I lost touch with most of them."

"You weren't going to school?" Kenny says. "How come?"

"I was having trouble with some of the girls," I say. "They bullied me for not fitting in. For being in care."

"That's so bad," Kenny says. "How much school did you miss?"

"About four months, I think. I was trying to do school work at home, but things were hard." I think of Mary and the arguments we had about me and Stephanie not getting on. I started to refuse to go to school and Stephanie teased me for that, even when she knew her friends were giving me grief too. I remember how Mary begged me to "try to get on with them" – and got upset when I refused.

Kenny sits down on the floor next to me. "I get that," he says. "I would be totally upset if I couldn't go to school." He pushes up his glasses and sighs. "I had hassle too, especially in Year Seven and a bit of Year Eight. I guess it's never cool to be a geek, is it?"

"Only to some people," I mutter. "But they don't matter."

Kenny points at the laptop. "Is there anything you need help with on here? Anything you'd like to be able to do?"

"I'm not sure," I say, pausing. "Maybe we could look up my home town? Where I used to live with my nan?"

It doesn't take long for Kenny to do it, and soon he is whisking us down the streets of Nan's town. A familiar feeling spins inside me. It's like I am a little girl again, walking down these streets. Seeing the old sights, the church on the corner. My old primary school. It's like going back in time.

I point at the screen. "That's it. That's my nan's house."

I can hardly believe it, seeing the house on screen all of a sudden. It looks different somehow – not like the house I lived in for so long.

"So, this is a house you lived in before?" Kenny asks.

"Yeah, I lived there with my nan until I was six."

He frowns. "How come you left?"

"Nan got ill," I say. "Really ill." I keep staring at the screen. I found her right there, in her house, in the kitchen, curled up on the floor like a baby. "Nan had a bleed on the brain, the doctors said. It was massive. She died straight away."

Kenny drew in a sharp breath. "Amy. That's awful – and that's why you ended up ..."

He can't finish the sentence. I've noticed people hate saying the words, unless they mean them in a nasty way.

"That's how I ended up in care, yes," I say. I finally pull my gaze away from the laptop and look at Kenny. His cheeks are red and he's looking back at me nervously, like he doesn't know what to say next. "I didn't have any other family," I explain. "My mum ran off when I was a baby, and she was an only child. I have no clue who my dad is."

"And they can't find your mum?" Kenny asks.

I shrug. "I think the social workers tried, after Nan died, but they didn't get anywhere. Apparently she was in a bad way when she left, into drinking and drugs. I don't think she would ever be fit to be a parent."

"That's terrible," Kenny says. "I can't even imagine what it must've felt like, losing your nan like that and then having no one else."

I lower my gaze as I reply. "It was awful. I felt lost, I suppose. I didn't belong anywhere any more."

"You must miss her, your nan?" Kenny asks.

"I do. A lot."

Kenny gently closes the laptop. "I hope you can be happy here," he says finally. "A new start, right?"

I smile back weakly. "I hope so too."

Later, I pick up my journal to write again. I could use the new laptop, of course. I think that's what Gemma meant for me to do. She probably saw my journal and thought that I write silly stories or notes in it. But it's far more important than that.

I can only write to Nan in here. Somehow, I know she will be listening.

Seeing your house again, Nan, made me remember all kinds of things. I'd forgotten just how small it was. I suppose I was smaller when I lived there, so the kitchen always seemed big. At Gemma and Graham's there is space everywhere. It's so different, not what I'm used to.

But they're nice. Gemma is sweet and Graham is funny. I like Kenny too – I just hope he doesn't get bored of me like Stephanie did. I'm too scared to get my hopes up, in case it all goes wrong again. I don't think I can face that.

I want this to work, Nan. I really do. But I'm just so scared.

Can I let myself believe this time will be different?

SEVEN

BEFORE

Mary and I were cooking together, making a pie for dinner. Mary was frying the chicken and vegetables, and I was rolling out the pastry. I did it carefully, making sure the pastry was smooth and even. As I worked, I thought of my nan. How she would use a milk bottle for a rolling pin and giggle that the cold glass hurt her hands if she did it for too long. If I really focused, I could hear Nan beside me. The throaty rasp of her laughter, the gentle sound of her humming.

"You look lost in thought." Mary's voice broke my thoughts.

I looked up. Mary was facing me, wiping her hands on her apron.

"Are you OK, Amy?" she asked. "How's school?"

I bowed my head a little. "It's OK – I suppose ..."

Mary cleared her throat and said, "I heard from your form tutor today. He said you didn't show up for afternoon registration."

I didn't reply.

"Where were you, Amy?" Mary asked.

"I ..." I hesitated. I looked up at Mary's wide eyes. I wanted to tell her how Stephanie and her friends had shoved me in the corridor at lunch. How they had jeered and called me names. I wanted to tell her how I had burst into tears in front of them.

What else could I do but run away from there? I just wanted to be on my own.

"Amy?" Mary's voice was soft. "You know I'm going to have to tell the social worker about this."

Mary's expression was gentle, but I could see the dark circles under her eyes. I'd heard her arguing with Stephanie the night before. They seemed to argue a lot more these days too.

"I had a headache," I said finally. "I'm sorry. I just wanted to get away."

"You should have gone to the medical room," Mary said. "Or phoned me."

"I know. I didn't think. I'm sorry ..."

Mary nodded. "Well, as long as you're sure that's all it is—"

"It is," I said.

"Because I know you are still struggling to get along with Stephanie." Mary sighed softly. "I've tried talking to Stephanie about this too. She tells me you're rude to her – and rude to her friends."

"I'm not," I replied sharply. "I just don't think Stephanie likes me much."

"Why? What has she said?" Mary asked.

I lowered my head. I didn't know what to say. Fear kept the words trapped in my throat. If I told Mary the truth, I wasn't sure she would believe me. And even if she did, how would Stephanie react? It would make things a million times worse.

"Is there anything you want to tell me, Amy?" Mary persisted.

"I'm fine, Mary," I whispered. "I just don't think me and Stephanie have much in common."

Mary studied me for a moment or two and then sighed. "I'll talk to Stephanie again. I'll ask her to try harder." She paused. "I can't have your school work start to suffer, Amy. I just hope things can settle down again between you two. That's what I hope."

I nodded again, tears pricking at my eyes. But I don't think Mary noticed. She went back to the hob and began stirring the pan.

But she had said the word twice – "hope", not "I know" or "I think".

But "I hope".

And that made me think she was starting to have doubts.

His door slams. I pick up my bag slowly. My stomach whips and swirls. I squeeze the handles of my bag together, wishing I could be somewhere else.

"It'll be OK, you know," Gemma says. "You wait and see. It'll go better than you think."

"You reckon?" I say.

"I reckon." Gemma nods and smiles. "And if not, I'm only a phone call away – OK?"

"OK," I reply.

But I feel very far from OK as I get out of the car. My legs are like jelly and my head is hurting.

This is about as far from OK as I can possibly be.

My form group is in a Maths room. Kenny shows me to the door. He peers in.

"It looks OK," he says. "Not everyone has arrived yet. Get in, introduce yourself. Try to relax."

"That sounds easier than it actually is," I say.

Kenny shrugs. "Don't overthink it. New girls are interesting. If you act cool and relaxed, everyone will want to be your friend." He pulls his bag over his shoulder. "Maybe I'll see you at lunch? Come and find me if you need to."

I watch as Kenny walks away, his head slightly lowered. He certainly doesn't look like one of the cool kids. In fact, I see a couple of older students push past him in the corridor, but Kenny gives the impression he doesn't care what people think. I decide I like that about him.

I walk into the room, trying to ignore everyone's eyes suddenly turning to me. Some of the desks are taken. People are spread out, sitting on the tables or on the chairs, which are turned in so they are all facing each other. I can see one free desk and it's right at the front of the room. I make my way slowly towards it.

"Hi," I say to one of the girls sitting nearby. "Does anyone sit here?"

"No. Not normally," she says, looking up at me, interested. "Hey. Are you new?"

"Yeah." I manage a smile. "I'm Amy."

The girl smiles. She is small and pretty with dark straight hair cut into a sharp bob. "Welcome. I'm Demi," she says. "This is my friend Tia." Demi nudges the girl next to her.

Tia looks me up and down and then asks me, "So – where are you from originally?"

"I lived in Slatesbourne," I say.

Tia frowns a bit. "That's miles away. Did your parents move or something?"

"No." I sit down, feeling heavy. I hate all these questions. "My nan died and I lived with someone else for a while."

"Aw, that's sad," says Demi. "Poor you."

I feel my cheeks burn. I don't want people to feel sorry for me. That's not what I asked for.

"I'm fine actually," I snap. "I'm not a poor anything."

"Oh!" Tia says. "Friendly, aren't you?"

"I was only trying to be polite," Demi says, looking hurt. Tia squeezes her arm and glares at me. I feel awful and start to apologise, but then Tia speaks again.

"Maybe you shouldn't bother with the new girl, Demi. Looks like she has an attitude problem."

"I haven't—" I start to say.

Tia holds out her hand. "No. Don't worry," she says smoothly. "We'll not bother you again."

She nudges Demi to join in with the rest of the group and they turn away from me.

I've been at school ten minutes and I've already managed to upset the first people I've spoken to. So far this is going as badly as I'd feared.

I drift through the first two classes, nodding numbly as teachers introduce me in each class and watching as the class stare back at me. A few girls try to speak to me, and I'm polite but I don't say much. I don't want to risk upsetting anyone again. It seems far easier to keep my head down and my mouth closed. I hear some people whisper behind me. I'm not sure if they're talking about me or not, but I'm guessing there is a good chance they are.

I slip into the toilets at break and lock the door of the cubicle. I feel safe in here, shut away from the huge loud crowds. But it isn't long before I hear the bathroom door crash open, a group of girls rushing in. At first they talk loudly about some boy who followed them down the corridor and they giggle. Then one of the girls says how rubbish Mr Frazer's German classes are. My ears prick up. That was my last lesson.

"I hate him so much," the girl continues. I don't recognise her voice, but I'm guessing she's from the group of girls who sat together in a small pack at the back of the classroom. "He talks too fast and he always picks on us."

Yes, it has to be them. Mr Frazer kept picking on them for answers. The loudest and prettiest of the group was a girl called Ashley. I wonder if it's her talking.

"Aw, Ash, I reckon it's only because he knows you're good at it," someone replies.

Ah! Right again.

"Did you see that new girl? How weird was she?"

My back stiffens. I press myself up against the cubicle wall, wishing I could vanish.

"Yeah, she won't talk to anyone," says another voice. "Really moody. Is she snobby or what?"

There's a giggle. "No way. I heard she's living with Kenny Dawson."

"What, Kenny in Year Ten?"

"Yeah. And you know he was telling everyone about his parents taking in a foster kid."

Thanks, Kenny.

"Aw." This sounds like Ashley again. "The poor cow is in care then? Probably has a drugged-up mum or dad. No wonder she looks so sad."

"Might want to stay out of her way then? She could be trouble."

They all screech with laughter and then clatter back out of the toilets. Leaving me behind. Standing in my stupid cubicle feeling smaller than ever.

Everyone will know now. They'll know I'm in care.

They'll all know there is something wrong with me.

I'm not sure how I make it through the rest of the morning. It's really hard to focus and I feel like everyone's eyes are on me. Is it my imagination or do the teachers seem to be studying me too? I wonder what they think of me. They must have seen my notes. They will know my background. It makes me even more angry that they might feel sorry for me, so I bend my head over my books and refuse to answer any questions, even when I know the answers.

Today is about hiding and getting through – nothing more.

I'm briefly relieved when the lunch bell goes. Gemma told me that she loaded my lunch card with money, so I know I can buy whatever I want. I'm not really hungry, but I walk quickly to the dinner hall as it seems the right place to be. I don't even have to worry about going the wrong way – the swirling crowds lead me there.

It's busier inside and even louder. This is probably the biggest dining area I've ever been in. The queue for the hot food already snakes halfway round the room, so I choose to join the short queue for cold food instead. I pluck a dry-looking sandwich and packet of fruit from the fridge and wait. All around me, people are talking and laughing. I feel so exposed standing here on my own. It's a relief to reach the front of the queue and ram my card under the digital reader.

I look around me. There is nowhere to sit. All the tables are full and crowded. I see Demi and Tia from this morning sitting at the back on a long table. Not knowing what else to do, I drift over. Then I realise Ashley and her friends are sitting there too.

They all look up as I walk over, their bright faces blinking at me. They don't say anything, and Demi even smiles at me, but something thunders inside me. I remember what I overheard in the toilets and my head feels hot. Suddenly I do not want to be there with them. They will ask questions. They will judge me.

I turn around.

I hear one of them suck her teeth. "See. She's so moody."

"Yeah – what was that even about?"

I want to tell them that I'm not moody. I'm just scared. I don't even know what I would say if I sat with them. How would I ever fit in? I'm kidding myself ever thinking I could.

Tears are stinging my eyes. I look around. There is nowhere else to sit. This place is too full, too loud. I need to get out.

I'm just about to walk away when someone touches my arm. I freeze and then twist my body. Kenny is standing behind me.

"Hey," he says. "You OK? How was your morning?"

I stare back at him. I don't know how to answer. I'm standing there holding my food, feeling miserable and lonely. I can't tell Kenny how awful my morning was and yet I can't bring myself to lie to him. My tongue is stuck in my mouth.

Kenny's eyebrow lifts a little and he looks backwards at the table he's just stood up from. "Never mind," he says. "Why don't you come and sit with us for a bit?"

My eyes widen. I can't help it. "You don't mind?" I say.

I glance at his table. I'm guessing this group are older: Year Tens, probably. A mixture of boys and girls. One of them smiles at me – a girl with long hair so dark it looks blue. I begin to relax.

"Of course not," Kenny says casually. "What's family for?"

EIGHT

BEFORE

Stephanie caught up with me on the school playground. It was the day after I'd spoken to Mary in the kitchen. Stephanie's face was twisted into a sneer and her eyes blazed with a cool force that made me look away. Behind her stood a huddle of friends, whispering and giggling. I tried to turn away, sensing trouble, but it was too late. She wasn't going to let me go.

"What did you say to my mum?" Stephanie said. "She was on my case last night! Telling me I have to try to be nicer to you."

The girls laughed harder. I didn't speak.

"What is it about you?" Stephanie demanded, pushing forward. "Why do you keep clinging on to Mum like some kind of sad loser? Do you really think she wants to hear your problems?"

"She was asking me ..." I stammered. "She kept asking. I didn't say anything really. I just told her that I didn't think you liked me."

Stephanie snorted. "Well, that's true."

"Your mum wanted to help," I said. "She wants me to be happy."

Stephanie laughed. "No. She doesn't." Her words cut into me, like a knife to my stomach. "She just feels sorry for you. Is that what you want? For everyone to feel sorry for you?" She laughed – it was a hollow, hard sound. "You know, I was actually excited about you coming. I thought you'd be fun. Interesting maybe, but instead all you want to do ..."

"What?" I whispered, barely able to challenge her. "What do I want to do?"

"You want my mum," Stephanie shot back. "And I told you before, it's not happening."

"I—"

"We were better off without you," she hissed. "You never should have come."

NOW

Kenny sits down next to me at the dining table and introduces me to the group sitting with him. "This is Dan, James, Ellen and Kelly."

I smile shyly at them and say, "Hi."

"Was everything OK? You looked a bit wound up," Kenny says.

I start to open my sandwich, still feeling really awkward. "It's just been a stressful morning. I've not found it that easy."

Kelly leans forward. She's the girl with the dark hair. "First days are always tough," she says. "Don't stress, you'll get used to it."

"I should be used to it by now," I say. "I had to go to two primary schools and a different secondary school before this one."

"It still doesn't make it easy, does it?" Kelly says gently. "Kenny was telling us about you. He told us that you moved in recently."

I feel my cheeks get hot, but Kenny nudges me and says, "It's cool, Amy. These guys understand."

Dan leans forward now. He has floppy blond hair and a lazy smile. "It's no big deal to us," he says. "I was in care for a bit, with Ellen."

I glance over at Ellen. I see their similar smiles and large eyes. They must be brother and sister.

"Yeah, I'm Year Eight too," Ellen says. "But I don't think I'm in any of your classes, which is a shame." Her smile widens. "But you can still sit with us at lunch and breaktime. I know what the girls can be like. They're nosy, that's all. They'll soon lose interest once something else comes along."

"You think?" I say, feeling a dart of hope.

"Sure." Ellen sits back, looking relaxed. "It was hard for me and Dan for a while. There were all these rumours going around school that our parents were some kind of psychos, that they couldn't take care of us." She shakes her head.

"It was pretty difficult to deal with at the time, but we did."

"We were in a care home for a while until things got better at home," Dan says quietly. "I mean, it's still not perfect now. We have social workers checking on us all the time and there are still … problems. But it's OK."

"School is fine most of the time," Ellen says firmly. "In fact, sometimes it can help."

I feel so warm inside. It's like all the icy walls I built around myself are melting away at last.

Kenny turns towards me. "There are people here who understand," he says.

"Yeah," says Kelly. "We're not all so bad."

I take a bite of my sandwich. I can finally eat and start to relax. The sounds of the dinner hall don't seem so loud any more, and at our table I allow myself to sit back and listen to the rest of the conversation. I even join in at times, sharing some of my experiences of my last school, being at the Gibsons' and some of the friends I had before. It's not so bad, opening up. In fact, it's refreshing.

By the time the bell goes again, I feel so much lighter.

The afternoon passes much faster. The last lesson is English, my favourite, and I end up sitting next to a girl called Hannah. She is quiet at first but still friendly. We have to work together on a comprehension piece, and I discover she is actually pretty funny and makes jokes about the work.

"I hate Shakespeare," Hannah tells me, pulling a face.

"Really? Oh, he's not so bad," I say. I don't admit to her that *Romeo and Juliet*, the play we are studying, is my absolute favourite. I don't want Hannah to think I'm a total geek.

"How are you finding it here?" she asks as the lesson comes to an end. "Have you made many friends?"

I think of lunchtime and shrug. "I guess I'm getting there."

Hannah grins. "Well, maybe we should hang out sometime," she says. "I can introduce you to a few people." She gives me her number. "Message me. We'll sort something out."

The bell rings and I nod at her. "Yeah, that'll be great."

Maybe today hasn't been quite as bad as I thought.

Gemma told me to meet Kenny after school. Although she drove us in this morning, I think she would like me and Kenny to walk to and from school together in future. I find Kenny waiting by the main entrance. He is flicking through a huge book. He holds it up as I approach.

"It's about Python," Kenny says. "I borrowed it from the library. It should keep me busy."

I look at him blankly. He might as well be speaking another language.

"Coding," he says. "Python is just another method. I need to get better at it."

"OK." I nod.

We start walking down the main road out of school. It's pretty busy with parents picking kids up and groups gathering together. We have to weave our way between the crowds.

"It's not far," Kenny says. "We'll take a shortcut through the park."

I don't know the town that well, but it seems pretty small. You could probably get to most places within half an hour.

"Have you always lived here?" I ask Kenny.

He nods. "Yeah. I guess that's kind of boring?"

I pull a face, thinking about this. "I dunno," I say. "I think it's kind of nice to stay in one place."

I know the one place I would have stayed if I could.

If I'd ever had a choice.

We walk down the street towards the house. I'm still getting used to how nice this part of town is.

"It must have been quiet growing up here," I say. "No trouble at all?"

Kenny hitches up his bag higher. "I guess." He looks over at me. "What was the last place you lived at like – the Gibsons'?"

"Well, it was much bigger than my nan's house," I say. "But it always felt more cramped because they had lots of stuff. Collectables and things. But it was OK – I had my own room, and the house faced a green, so I could play outside."

"And that was the main home you lived in after your nan's?" Kenny asks.

I flinch a bit – I can't help it. "There were a few other places first. One didn't work out and the others were only temporary."

Kenny nods. "And the Gibsons were meant to be permanent?"

"Yeah."

The burning feeling returns to the pit of my stomach. I know Kenny doesn't mean to upset me, but I hate going over these things again. It never gets any easier.

"So what—" Kenny begins, but sees my face and stops walking. He holds out his hands as if to say sorry. "Do you know what? You don't have to tell me. I'm being really nosy, I know."

"No, it's OK." I lower my head so I don't have to meet his intense stare. "I mean, I don't really like talking about it, but it's OK to ask. The truth is the Gibsons didn't want me there any more. My foster mum, Mary, made up some excuse about not being well, but I'm not sure I believe that. It was too stressful for her. I used to argue all the time with her daughter, Stephanie. We really didn't get on – Stephanie knew how to wind me up. I knew Mary couldn't handle it any longer."

"Oh," Kenny says. "That sounds harsh."

"Mary wants to stay in touch and stuff," I tell him. "My social worker said I should, but I can't face it."

"Do you think there's more to it? Maybe Mary feels bad about what happened?"

"I doubt that," I say.

"But surely if—"

"No!" I snap. "Mary made her choice and I made mine. That's the end of it."

We walk in silence. Kenny tries to restart the conversation, but I don't bother answering. I'm too tired. I just want to get back to the house and shut myself away again.

The truth is that the breakdown of the Gibson placement really shook me up. I really hoped that it would be my forever home. I wanted it to work out between me and Stephanie and I still do not know what I did to upset her so much.

I think that's what really gets to me. The confusion. The fact that I can never truly understand what I did wrong. And if I can't understand that, how can I stop it from happening again?

As we approach the Dawsons' house, my heart tilts a little. Could it really be different here? Could I really allow myself to believe that this is my new home?

As we go into the house, I hear Gemma on the phone in the living room. I turn to Kenny and indicate that we need to be quiet. He nods and gently closes the front door.

We pad towards the kitchen. Kenny is now ahead of me – he's already rummaging around in the fridge looking for something to eat. I can hear Gemma loud and clear. Her voice is so bright and sharp it would be difficult not to listen.

When I hear her say my name, I freeze. It's like I'm trapped there in the kitchen doorway, having to hear Gemma's words. I should walk away of course, but I don't. I stand there instead and make myself listen.

"Yeah ... I know," Gemma says. "That's exactly what I was saying to Graham last night."

Her voice has lowered slightly, so I creep back towards the open door of the living room. My body feels stiff and heavy. I'm so scared I'll make a noise. I stand between the open door and the staircase and continue to listen in. I feel bad doing this. It's nosy, isn't it? It's wrong. But at the same time, Gemma's talking about me. Surely I have a right to know what she's saying?

"Like I say, we discussed this together, Clare." Gemma's voice is quiet now. "I'm really sorry, but we can't go forward with the placement. It won't work for our family. I have to consider us all in this."

I'm not even sure how I make it up the stairs, but I do. I tread carefully, even though my feet feel like they're made of lead. Sickness gurgles in my stomach and my head is spinning.

They don't want me. They don't want to go forward with the placement.

I don't work for the family.

Their family.

I stagger into my room – except it's not my room, is it? For a moment, I simply stand in the space, looking around me, wondering how on earth I could've thought that this would work. Downstairs I hear the sound of Kenny and Gemma talking in the kitchen. She is off the phone now. I wonder if they even know where I am.

Where even am I?

Where will I go now?

I only ever belonged in one place and that wasn't at the Gibsons' and it's clearly not here either.

I walk over to the wardrobe, quickly pack my bag and then shove it under the bed. I will wait. I will wait until this evening, until everyone is distracted by TV and computers, and then I will leave.

I will go back to the only place I have ever belonged. Where I can't be rejected and moved on again.

I'll go back to my only home.

NINE

BEFORE

I was writing in my journal when Stephanie came in. All I wanted to do was talk to Nan again, to tell her how I was feeling and how much I missed her. I just wanted five minutes on my own to get my head together and stop my upsetting thoughts from taking over. But Stephanie couldn't even give me that.

"What you doing?" she asked.

Her voice broke my focus. I looked up to see Stephanie standing in my doorway, her expression a mixture of curiosity and smugness.

"Nothing," I said, and tried to slide the journal under my duvet.

"What's that ... What are you trying to hide from me?" Stephanie strode towards the bed. "Oh my God, is that actually a diary?"

"No," I said. "It's not."

"It is." She smirked. "You've got a diary, haven't you? Let me see. I bet you've been bitching all about me."

Stephanie shoved me, which surprised me, as she'd never been physical before. She was as fast as a cat, grabbing my book and turning away from me, clasping it to her chest so I couldn't reach.

"Give it back!" I yelled.

"Oh no ..." Stephanie's fingers began to poke at the pages. "I want to see what you have to say ... What's this? Oh ... Stephanie winds me up. She's mean all the time ..." Her eyes widened and she laughed. "Oh, Amy. What have you been saying about me? This isn't nice at all ... What will my mum say?"

I could feel the heat rising in my body. "Give it back!"

"And who is this you're talking to? Oh my God – it's your nan." Stephanie laughed again.

"You're writing to your old dead nan. How sad are you?"

It was at that moment the world turned red.

NOW

I stay in my room, waiting for the right time. Gemma pops her head in to see me. She asks if I'm OK, but I tell her I have a headache and I want to rest. I think she sees my pale face and believes me. Gemma asks if I want any food, but I tell her I feel too sick.

A bit later, Graham brings up a plate of sandwiches and crisps anyway. He tells me to eat what I can manage. I can hardly stand to look at his face, even though he's smiling kindly. I wonder if he just feels sorry for me. Maybe they all do. I wonder when they are planning to tell me their decision.

At least I can save them the trouble now.

*

It's much later when I slip out of the house, and quieter too. I wait until Kenny is shut away in his room and Gemma and Graham are settled in front of a film downstairs. I put some music on in my room and put the cushions under the duvet so it looks like my body is snuggled under there.

Getting out is a little harder. I pick up the bag I packed and I also take the sandwiches that Graham gave me – I might need them later. I have to chuck my bag out of the window first, and then ease my body through the tight gap. Luckily my window overlooks the back kitchen extension, so I have a nice flat surface to land on. From there I jump neatly into the garden and then make my way out of the side gate.

I am out. I am gone.

I have enough money to get the night bus back to Slatesbourne, and that is where I am heading.

There is no point being here now. Unwanted. I can't stand the thought of being moved on again. Who knows what would be next for me? Another care home? Another temporary foster placement? Another family promising me a permanent home? I don't think I have the energy to deal with it all again.

I know the truth. I have known it for too long now.

I am alone in this world.

There's only one place I've ever really belonged.

I get on the night bus two streets away. The driver hardly looks at me as I pay my money and shuffle to the back of the bus. I try not to look at him just in case. I know Gemma and Graham will have to report me missing when they see I'm gone. They might even get into trouble for letting me escape. I wonder if they'll be angry with me.

I slump in my seat and take out my phone. I feel so tired and worn out by everything. It's like I'm crumbling inside. I wonder how I will ever find my energy again. I don't have any real plans. I don't have any clue as to how I can get more money or keep myself alive. But all I can hear is the little voice in my head that won't shut up. It's telling me that I will never be happy, that I have to keep running and not trust people again. I have to get used to being by myself.

I swipe through the pictures on my phone. They are mainly of old friends, people I don't even see any more. Previous lives that I've had to leave behind. As I scan back, I find photos of the Gibsons – of the family that was meant to be mine. I see a photo of Mary with her face pressed up to mine. She is smiling but I can see how tired her face is, the dark shadows dancing under her eyes. Was she really as ill as she said? Or did I make her ill with my constant arguing with Stephanie? Could Mary really no longer cope?

I swipe back further and my head spins as I stare at the photos. I didn't look at these for so long because they hurt me too much, but now I can't tear my eyes away from them. My mind whirls as I swipe.

What did I do wrong this time? Why doesn't Gemma want me? Am I too quiet? Too grumpy? Am I not the sort of girl she is looking for?

Or perhaps it's Kenny? Maybe he doesn't like me? Maybe he was only pretending to be nice?

Am I really that hard to like?

My finger stops swiping. I have come across an older photo, taken long ago but sent to this phone when I first got it. It's an image of an original photograph. You can see the creases on the paper. The reflection of the light hitting the faces. But it doesn't matter. It's precious. It's of my nan and me.

I stare at it.

I remember it being taken. Nan's neighbour, Mrs Harris, had invited us to some party. She was the one who had sent me the photograph. I don't even know if she still lives next door to my nan's house, but they used to be best friends.

I think I'm about four in the photo. My face is covered in cream from the cake I've just eaten, and my hair is tied up in bunches. Nan is carrying me on her hip. Her face is turned towards me. Her greyish blonde hair is loose and bouncy around her face, her mouth is open in a laugh. Nan looks so happy.

We both do.

I trace the picture with my finger, a stinging memory coming back – of being wanted, being held. Nan whispering in my ear that she loved me and would be there for me for ever.

It's not fair. None of this is fair.

How did it go so wrong?

Why did she have to leave me?

When the bus pulls into my old town, I stagger towards the door. My legs are wobbly and my head hurts. I clutch my phone in my hands. Nan's picture is now saved as my screensaver. I will not hide it again. I need it with me.

"Are you all right, love?" the driver asks as I move towards the door. The bus is empty now and it seems he's finally noticed me here on my own.

"I'm fine," I say back, as bright as I can.

"Do you have somewhere to go?" the driver asks, frowning at me.

"Oh yes." I smile back, my fingers stroking my phone. "I'm going to my nan's."

She'll look after me.

She always did.

TEN

BEFORE

I rushed at Stephanie, who was still holding my
journal and laughing. I felt a huge surge of anger
and energy. I wanted my journal back. And I
wanted to stop her talking, that was all.

I just wanted to shut her up.

Stephanie moved out of my room and onto
the landing. She was still reading my journal and
giggling at the words.

"I miss you so much, Nan ..." she said, putting
on a silly, mocking voice. "Oh, Nan ... it's so hard.
Will I ever be happy again ...?"

"Give it to me!" I yelled.

I reached forward. I wanted to grab my book, but Stephanie pushed me away. Without thinking, I rushed towards her. Rage was growing like an uncontrollable wave inside me. I couldn't stop it.

I pushed Stephanie back. My strength surprised both of us. I saw her mouth open in shock.

Everything seemed to go in slow motion. I saw her head tip back, her arms flail as she tried to regain her balance, but she was falling backwards in nothingness.

Stephanie's cry was loud and piercing. I tried to grab her. I really did, but it was too late. She was already falling backwards down the stairs.

When I looked again, she was like a broken doll, curled up by the bottom step.

I couldn't move. I couldn't speak. Guilt froze me on the spot.

And then Mary came. She rushed to her daughter, crouched by her side and gently touched her hair.

Then she looked up at me. Her eyes were horrified. Her entire body was shaking.

"Amy – oh my God!" Mary said. "What have you done?"

NOW

Nan's house looks so different now, and yet so familiar. I immediately see a "for sale" sign that stands at an angle in the front garden and my throat tightens. I know other people must have lived there after Nan died, and now it looks like someone else will move in soon. But still, now that I'm here, the thought of anyone else living here makes me feel sick. This is my nan's house. Only hers.

I walk down the path, trying not to get upset by the fact the front door has been painted a new colour and the lawn is paved over. I peer in through the front window. I can see its empty inside. At least no one is there now.

I hate change. It claws at me. It makes me remember all the things I have lost and will never get back. But one thing hasn't changed and that's Nan's funny stone goblin by the side gate. I approach him carefully, hardly able to believe that he's still there. His wise, ugly face smiles at me. Nan used to pat his head on her way out of the house. She called him Gordon and said he was her lucky charm.

"Hello, you," I whisper to him. I feel like I'm greeting an old friend.

There's another thing that hasn't changed. I gently tip the goblin's body away from me and see that Nan's spare key is still underneath him. The key is embedded in the earth and rusty, but it's there waiting for me. I'm so thankful. It's a sign, I'm sure it is. I'm doing the right thing.

I'm home again.

It's cold inside the house and smells musty, but I don't care. I walk into the hall and take a shaky breath. If I squeeze my eyes half shut, I can imagine Nan standing here with me, her hand leading me up the stairs to bed. Her voice is soft as she sings a nursery song ...

Hush, little baby, don't say a word,
Mamma's going to buy you a mockingbird ...

How is it possible that I can hear Nan's voice now, as if she's here beside me? I can smell her rich floral perfume. I can feel the soft folds of her long skirt as it brushes me.

"Oh, Nan," I whisper.

I sit on the bottom step and rest my head against the wall. Now that I'm here I realise that I can't go any further. I do not want to go into the kitchen – the memories there are too awful to relive. I do not want to go upstairs and find the empty rooms there – reminding me that my dear nan will never come back.

So instead, I stay here. On the stairs. Halfway between the past and present. Stuck in a loop that never seems to end.

"Nan …" I whisper again. "Nan, it all went so wrong. Why did that happen?"

I reach inside my bag. I need my journal. I need to write my thoughts down, to tell Nan how I'm feeling. But as I dig around inside, it's clear I left my journal behind.

My journal!

"Nan …" I say, my voice cracking. "Nan, I messed up badly. I don't know what to do."

And then I begin to cry.

The Gibsons. It should have worked. It really should've been my forever home, and maybe it would've been if I had been stronger. Should I have told Mary the truth, that her daughter was a bully? Should I have tried harder to work things out with Stephanie?

I didn't mean to push Stephanie. I didn't mean for her to fall down the stairs. I certainly didn't mean for her to break her ankle – but all these things happened.

Stephanie later said it was all my fault. She told Mary that it was me bullying her and that I made her life miserable.

There was no point arguing against Stephanie. I decided that no one would believe me, the broken kid in foster care. I was the outsider. What was the point anyway? Stephanie would never like me – things would never change. I was pretty sure I couldn't be happy there.

Mary changed after the accident. I saw how tired she looked, how she struggled to make eye contact with me. She said soon after that she was too ill to foster, but I knew it was a lie.

Mary just no longer wanted me.

She gave up.

I think I sleep for a bit, slumped on the stairs. I wake up to my neck aching and my head throbbing. In my bag I can hear the soft pulse of my phone buzzing. I pull it out and see that I have missed calls from Gemma and my social worker. I ignore them and quickly turn my phone off.

I don't want to hear Gemma's excuses. I don't want to be told all the reasons the Dawsons don't want to keep me.

I walk into the living room.

It's so cold and empty in here now, and so different. I long to see Nan's old furniture, her favourite chair, the large TV in the corner of the room. It's all gone. It's all too different.

My stomach growls with hunger and my body aches. I sit on the hard, uncarpeted wooden floor and bring my knees up to my chest.

I don't know what to do any more.

It's later, much later. It's dark now. I can hear banging on the door.

I bring my legs tighter to my chest. My heart is thumping so hard I think it might burst out.

I squeeze my eyes shut.

The letterbox flaps open.

"Amy?"

It's Gemma. My stomach flips inside me. How did she know I was here?

"Amy, are you there?" Gemma says. "If you are, please come to the door."

Go away, I think.

I don't want to see her.

"Amy ..." Gemma's voice breaks. "Please be there, please. We are all so worried. If you're not here, I don't know what to do ..."

I shift on the spot. There is something in her voice. Something I haven't heard before. She sounds so desperate, so upset.

"Kenny thought you might be here," Gemma goes on. "He worked it out. He's so worried. We all are." She pauses. "Amy, Kenny thinks you heard me on the phone. Did you? Were you listening? I think you might've got things wrong. Please open the door so I can explain. Please be there. We can't be wrong about this."

I get up slowly. I'm unsure. I don't know what to do. My head is spinning.

Gemma keeps talking, her voice wobbling now.

"When you heard me talking on the phone, it wasn't about you. It wasn't, Amy. The social workers wanted me to take on another foster child and I wasn't ready."

Another child … My ears prick up. They were talking to Gemma about another child. She was turning down another placement. Not me.

"I said no because I didn't think I was ready," Gemma continues. "I didn't think my family was. And by family, I was including you, Amy. You are part of our family now. You are important. I want you to know that. You are as important to us as anyone. I want you home with us. Your family."

Family.

Gemma wanted me. She really did.

"Amy ..." Her voice is so gentle. "Amy. We want you. We really do. We want you. You belong with us. We want you to come home."

Slowly and very carefully, I pick myself up. Then, before any doubt gets to me, I walk towards the door.

"I'm coming," I whisper. "I'm coming home."

AFTER

Months pass.

I could lie and tell you everything was perfect for me after that, but what would be the point? The truth is we all had to work at getting things right, like with most things. I can still be quiet at times and push people away.

I still find school tricky, and at first I hung around with Kenny and his mates. But as time passed, I found I could trust some of the girls in my year. I got closer to Ellen and Hannah – I opened up a little. I guess I started to believe that I was here to stay – and that helped. I let myself make friends. And yeah, I still get grief from some of the kids in my year, but I'm learning to ignore it. I know I can't help my past. It's part of who I am, and if people can't accept that about me – well, that's their problem!

I've spent more time with Gemma too. We do lots of baking together. She seems to understand that my moods are up and down and that it takes me a long time to build trust. Gemma says that's OK. She says the one thing we have is time and that there is no rush. We talk a lot and it is helping. She got me a frame to put Nan's picture in. It sits by my bed, next to a brand-new journal that I write in every night.

It helps to see Nan's smiley face every day. I think she would be pleased to see me here. I think she would be relieved to see me trying my best and looking to the future finally, rather than focusing on the past.

I still miss Nan badly, of course, and part of me always will. But I think I've realised now that it is possible to belong somewhere again.

Gemma also made me speak to Clare, my social worker, about my experience at the Gibsons. Gemma and Clare both told me that I shouldn't be blaming myself for things not working out there. When Clare took over my case, she thought my previous social worker had already talked to me about what had happened. Clare didn't realise I hadn't been told the full details. She explained that the placement hadn't broken down just because of my behaviour – but also because of Stephanie's.

Nobody realised how much Stephanie had struggled with the placement. But they know now that my arrival had made her feel insecure and her anxiety had risen. She had been unable to cope with sharing so much of her life with me. Mary had felt it wasn't fair on either of us for the placement to continue and was worried that we were both suffering. Mary wasn't cross at me for that final incident on the stairs, but it made her realise it wasn't working.

And Mary *was* ill, that hadn't been a lie. Her illness and Stephanie's behaviour had made them decide to end the placement. Stephanie is getting help now too, and Mary says she regrets everything she put me through. I believe her.

At the time I was so upset and confused that I convinced myself it was all my fault. But now I can see it wasn't. I guess sometimes things just don't work out the way you hope they will.

So, I understand now. I'm still disappointed that the placement went wrong, but at least I know it wasn't all about me. I'm learning to try not to get so upset about the things I can't change and to focus on the stuff I can.

I have a counsellor who helps me. I see her once a week. I think she's helping me untangle the negative thoughts in my head. She's helping me to see all the good things in my life. And there are lots. In many ways I know I am lucky.

So, yeah. It's not a "happy ever after" for me, but it's a "*happier* ever after". And you know what? I'm OK with that.

I'm just glad to be settled.

This is my home. My place.

And it feels good.

EVE AINSWORTH

BECAUSE

OF

YOU

JUST
ANOTHER
LITTLE
LIE

EVE AINSWORTH

ISBN: 978-1-78112-867-1

ISBN: 978-1-78112-911-1

ALSO BY

Eve Ainsworth

Our books are tested
for children and young people by
children and young people.

Thanks to everyone who consulted on
a manuscript for their time and effort in
helping us to make our books better
for our readers.